Topic: Transportation and Safety **Subtopic:** Different Kinds of Transportation

Notes to Parents and Teachers:

At this level of reading, your child will rely less on the pattern of the words in the book and more on reading strategies to figure out the words in the story.

REMEMBER: PRAISE IS A GREAT MOTIVATOR!

Here are some praise points for beginning readers:

- You matched your finger to each word that you read!
- I like the way you used the picture to help you figure out that word.
- I noticed that you saw some sight words you knew how to read!

Book Ends for the Reader!

Here are some reminders before reading the text:

- Use picture clues to help figure out words.

- Get your mouth ready to say the first sound in a word and then stretch out the word by saying the sounds all the way through the word.

- Skip a word you do not know, and read the rest of a sentence to see what word would make sense in that sentence.

- Use sight words to help you figure out other words in the sentence.

Words to Know Before You Read

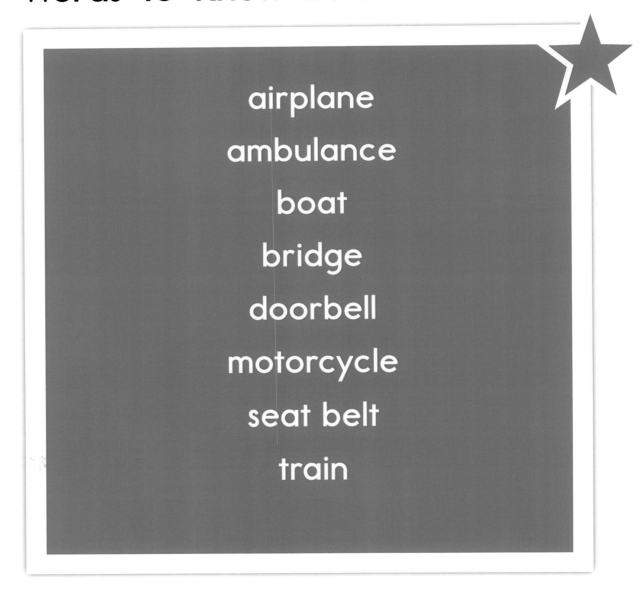

airplane

ambulance

boat

bridge

doorbell

motorcycle

seat belt

train

A LONG CAR RIDE

By Jenny Lamb

Illustrated by
Marcin Piwowarski

Rourke
Educational Media
rourkeeducationalmedia.com

Dad, where are we going?

We are going to Grandma's house.

Is your seat belt on?

Yes! That's the first thing I do.

I look out the window. I see an airplane in the sky.

The airplane is fast.

ZOOM!
ZOOM!

Dad hears a noise. He sees an ambulance in the mirror.

The ambulance's siren is on.

We go over a bridge. I see a boat in the water.

The boat blows its horn.

How long will it take to get there?
Why? Dad asked.

I really need to use
the bathroom!

We stop at a crossing. I see a train on the tracks.

The train goes by.

Something goes past our car. I see a motorcycle on the road.

The motorcycle is so loud.

Finally, we get to Grandma's house.

I ring the doorbell in a hurry. Can I use your bathroom, Grandma?

Book Ends for the Reader

I know...

1. What did Dad ask before he started the car?

2. What did they see in the sky?

3. What did they see in the water?

I think ...

1. What kind of transportation do you use the most?

2. Do you think we need transportation in our lives?

3. What is your favorite type of transportation?

Book Ends for the Reader

What happened in this book?

Look at each picture and talk about what happened in the story.

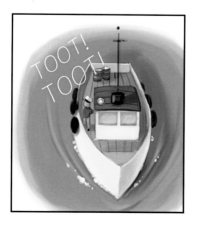

About the Author

Jenny Lamb graduated with a Master's degree in Journalism and International Business. She has written several books for young children and has a passion for mentoring and volunteering in schools in Colorado, where she lives with her dog, Nala. She enjoys traveling, reading, and cross country skiing.

About the Illustrator

Marcin Piwowarski is self-taught in traditional as well as digital illustration. He managed to make over one thousand books during his twenty-year artistic journey. As a single father of three kids, he understands what to include in his art for it to be adored and eye-catching.

Library of Congress PCN Data

A Long Car Ride / Jenny Lamb

ISBN 978-1-68342-728-5 (hard cover)(alk. paper)
ISBN 978-1-68342-780-3 (soft cover)
ISBN 978-1-68342-832-9 (e-Book)
Library of Congress Control Number: 2017935443

Rourke Educational Media
Printed in the United States of America, North Manchester, Indiana

www.rourkeeducationalmedia.com

Edited by: Debra Ankiel
Art direction and layout by: Rhea Magaro-Wallace
Cover and interior Illustrations by: Marcin Piwowarski